Barbara E

Puppy Dogs and Poo Bags

Illustrations by Melanie McIntyre

First Published in paperback in Great Britain in 2018

ISBN 978-9993068-0-9

Printed in England by Accent Commercial Resources,
Unit 10a, Sawley Park, Nottingham Road, Derby, DE7 6PJ.
www.accentcr.co.uk Tel: 01332 384420

Printed on FSC certified substrates from sustainable sources.

Email for orders and enquiries:
babs.everett@ntlworld.com

Email us about special pricing for schools, shelters and rescue organisations.

British Library Cataloguing in Publication Data.
A CIP catalogue record for this book is available from the British Library.

Contents

Thank you

I would like to thank my friends who helped me with this book. Melanie who did all of the brilliant illustrations at very short notice. Enid and Sharon (1) who have checked it over and over and over again. Also Maggie, Sue, Karen, Sylvia, Sharon (2), Stephanie and Kevin. Marie who helped structure my draft notes and her valid input. Julia, who came up with the brilliant title. Most importantly, Cooper, who inspired me to write this book - he is such a fun loving puppy. His Mum Sarah, for entrusting me with him every Tuesday, *as he is a live wire and goes bananas on the park!*

I would like to point out that this is the first time I have written a book! I am passionate about animals and just want to help people to realise what is involved in the decision to welcome a puppy ‘to be part of your family'. Also all the immense love, companionship, pleasure, fun and joy they bring to your family!
All animals are very precious and have feelings and emotions just like us, and they need our protection.

*****

For All God’s Creatures

1. Hello

Hello Boys and Girls,
I am very pleased to meet you. My name is Cooper and I have four brothers. Their names are Jack, Frank, Scott and Mason. We don't have any sisters but oh, I really would love a sister. That would be great!

Our Mum's coat is a creamy colour and Dad's is a rich brown, but all five of us were born with black coats! You would have thought that one of us would have taken after Mum or Dad, wouldn't you? Anyway, you would love our black curly coats, as they feel really soft, just like a little lamb's fleece.
Mum tells us that when we were born our eyes were closed and we suckled on her special milk, which helped us to become healthy and strong. When our tummies were full we would need to go to the toilet. Puppies don't wear nappies like babies do, so we tiddled and pooed on paper left down on the kitchen floor by our owners. Mum said that as we get older we will be trained to wee and poo in the garden, or when we are taken for a walk. So until then our owners have

to clean up after us, which they don't mind, because we are too young to understand.

We love to play fight and get tired quickly from running around. When we need a rest we all cuddle up together with Mum, and fall asleep and doggie dream for ages and ages and ages.......

We are all very happy and everyone who comes to see us loves us; in fact lots of people have been to visit us. There is one particular family, with two children, who come more often than the others. When they come I show off, rolling over on my back and prodding them with my paws, in the hope that they will play with me, and oh, we have so much fun together! The oldest member of the family is called 'Grandma'. She always has a twinkle in her eye and I get a feeling that she is very special and very kind. I often wonder as I drift off to sleep, what it would be like to go home with them.
For some reason this family gave me all the attention, which I loved, but my brothers, especially Mason the eldest, gave me strange looks. One day he even growled at me as we were all dozing off to sleep! This worried me, but Mum said he was just jealous, and because he was the biggest and eldest he thought he

was *Top Dog*, and should have got more attention than the rest of us. She told me to 'take no notice of him' so I did, and I didn't worry any more.

We were all growing very quickly and then, one day, we heard our Mum and Dad talking quietly saying that it would soon be time for us to leave.
But what did they mean? Where were we going?
My brothers and I couldn't understand so we talked amongst ourselves. Mason then had a word with Dad about what was going to happen, but when he came back he wouldn't speak, so we didn't know what was said. We could tell he wasn't happy, as he looked miserable and didn't eat, drink or sleep for a few days. So what was going on? It wasn't long after that, I remembered that feeling I had had about Grandma and her family, and each night before I fell asleep, I thought about the future.

Naturally, after eight weeks Mum was feeling exhausted from feeding five growing puppies. We were totally amazed where all Mum's milk came from, but we all agreed it tasted super and was very filling. Of course Mum always ate good healthy food which made her milk so great and nutritious, helping us to grow big and strong!

Our owners finally decided that we were now old enough at eight weeks to have solid food like our Mum and Dad. This was really exciting because their portions of food always looked and smelled very tasty and I noticed they always licked their bowls clean. That's always a good sign, isn't it?

I am really looking forward to this new food. I have noticed that occasionally Mum and Dad have a piece of apple after their meals. *I've heard it on the grapevine that, 'an apple a day keeps the doctor away'.* They also seem to like scrambled eggs with a little wholemeal toast. *I think I will like that!!*

2. A Knock at the Door

When we were ten weeks old, we were about to be given our bowl of food when there was a knock at the door. KNOCK… KNOCK… KNOCK… It was the grownups and Grandma (but no children). I followed them as they disappeared into another room, but they closed the door on me so I lay outside. I could hear them talking quietly and I got this funny feeling in my tummy that something was about to happen. I looked around to see that my brothers had followed me and were looking at me strangely.

Then Mason said, "I bet they have chosen you Cooper."
"Chosen me? What for?" I said.
"I bet it's you who is leaving us today," he muttered, sounding very fed up. "They only had eyes for you, we didn't stand a chance." But as he said this, he turned away in embarrassment and I'm sure I saw a little tear in his eye.

When the grown-ups eventually came out of the room they were looking at me! Grandma bent down and gently stroked me and put me on a lead. She then said,

“Come on Cooper off we go,” and we walked towards the door and down the path. My Mum and Dad ran along beside me, kissing and nudging me goodbye. My brothers also ran out and gave me lots of paw strokes; even Mason gave me a pat on the back!
Then Grandma picked me up and we got into the back of a shiny purple car.

As we drove away I looked back at the house where I was born and wondered *if I would ever see my ‘doggie family’ again?*
I will never-ever-forget seeing my big brother Mason with a 'tear in his eye'.

3. My First Car Ride

This is all new to me as I've never been in a car, it seemed to go very fast and things kept whizzing by.
My new owners sat in the front whilst I sat in the back on Grandma's knee. She held me very tight. I felt really safe, her arms were lovely and warm and her green woollen jumper was soft and cuddly. It reminded me of my Mum and I started to cry and tears rolled down my face. Grandma seemed to think it was the car that was frightening me, but I just wanted my Mum and Dad. I felt very small and alone so I curled up into a ball. I wished that I was back home with my brothers, even Mason.

The car stopped outside a big house. Grandma gently led me up the driveway. I was still feeling very tearful. Everywhere smelled different. I put my nose to the ground sniffing and crying at the same time, but soon we were at a big red door that opened and we went inside.

My new owners said, “Welcome to your new home Cooper, you are so cute! I wonder how big you are going to grow?"

Then everyone took their coats off and hung them up neatly in the hallway. *It’s very tidy here*, I thought. *What are they going to think if I wee or poo on the floor?*

4. Christmas Eve

It's Christmas Eve and I am taken into a nice big lounge where there is a real Christmas tree decorated with silver tinsel, baubles, and brightly lit with coloured fairy lights.

There's an empty cardboard box with holes in it on the floor and they put me inside. *What's going on?* I wondered.

Then I hear my new owner say, "The box isn't big enough!"

Grandma said, "I think it will be fine, he won't be in it for long, just make sure you don't cover the holes so he can breathe."

Oh dear, I think I am going to be someone's Christmas present and I'm not sure what I feel about this. All I know is that I have been placed in a box and the lights are shining through the holes.

I hear Grandma say, "He just fits inside the box nicely, and we can take him out now." So they lift me out. *Thank goodness for that,* I thought, *I am beginning to feel frightened.*

I think there must be children living here, I wonder if it is the children who used to visit my old house?

Then Grandma said, "Come on Cooper it's time to go outside." *Am I going to sleep in the garden?* I thought. I've never slept outside before and I started to get worried; however, there was nothing to worry about as I was just being taken out to go to the toilet before I go to bed. The new garden is fascinating, so many interesting smells for my nose to explore. I am so busy sniffing around that I forget to have a poo or a wee.

Back inside the house I am given a small bowl of tasty food and some water. A nice soft bed has been made for me in the big hallway, and I am so tired I just can't wait to get into it.

As the house falls silent and dark I start to feel lonely and think about my Mum, Dad and brothers. I wander around exploring my new home and WHOOPS!!! I do a wee and a poo in the living room! I start crying again and I can't stop. Everything is different and I want my old family back. I eventually cry myself to sleep. What a busy day I have had!

5. Christmas Day

All of a sudden I am woken up. *What's going on?* I thought. My new Dad is picking me up and putting me in that box again. It feels like the middle of the night but when I look at the clock it's 6 o'clock in the morning.
"Quick! the children will be awake soon and we need to put some tinsel and satin bows on the box before they come down," says Dad.
Then I hear Grandma say, "Don't forget, you mustn't cover the holes as he has got to be able to breathe."
Before long I hear footsteps on the stairs, it's dark and I'm feeling nervous.

"SANTA'S BEEN!!! SANTA'S BEEN!!!
He's eaten his mince pie, drank his sherry, and Rudolph has eaten his carrot!" I hear the children shout excitedly. "Santa and Rudolph must have been hungry with all their hard work, going up and down chimneys, delivering presents!"

I thought to myself *they are going to open their presents and find me very soon, so I can get out of this box!* I wait patiently and peer through the air holes, but they have other presents that they decide to open first! Oh dear, I'm desperate to get out….

A little while later, I hear Dad say, "Right kids – time to open the big present now! I don't know how Santa got this one down the chimney, but it looks a bit special to me, so be very careful how you open it."

The children gently open the box and there I am, nervously looking up at them with my big brown eyes and my black curly tail wagging.

THEY SSCCRREEAAMM WITH DELIGHT, pick me up, and cuddle me …… and in that moment I feel very loved and wanted. I get this warm feeling inside that I am going to be very happy here with my new family! I am so lucky!!

I am the centre of attention! Everyone is looking at me!! I feel very shy.
There are colourful ribbons, satin bows, paper, tinsel and presents scattered all around the room, and then I spot a small pile of unopened presents. *WOW! these look interesting and they've got my name on them.* I thought.
Dad saw me sniffing around and said, "Can someone open Cooper's presents for him, please?" The children rush to rip the paper off to reveal lots of goodies. WWWOOOWWWEEE!!!

- A diamante collar
- Stainless steel bowls with my name on them
- A safe 'ring tug toy' to chew on when I am teething
- A teddy bear
- Cotton towels for when I get smelly, wet and dirty
- A whistle – I wonder that's for?
- Poo bags – I wonder what they are for?

I wag my curly tail like mad to show my thanks, and in return I get lots of kisses and cuddles! I run and leap in the air with the excited children, who I learn are called Harry and Kate; they are my new brother and sister and I notice that they have as much energy as me, so living with them is going to be great! *At last I've got a sister!!* I thought.

"RRRIIIGGGHHHTTT," said Dad. "The first thing we have to do is to start training Cooper to be taken outside to have a wee and a poo, and don't forget the poo bags. To get him into a good routine you will have to do this every 2 to 4 hours."

So Dad showed Harry and Kate how to pick up my poo – he used a sausage to demonstrate!
"Put your hand inside the bag, pick up the sausage, then turn the bag inside out, tie it in a knot, and most importantly, put it in a bin… and don't forget to wash your hands!"
Harry and Kate looked at each other, grimacing.
Harry piped up, "I think that's your job Kate."
"Oh, No! Harry," she said. "Poo patrol is your job!"
"I don't want any arguing," said Mum. "You share it."

Harry and Kate spent the rest of the morning playing with me and their new toys. Dad had words with them about the toys that had batteries, especially the tiny ones. "They are *EXTREMELY DANGEROUS* if you swallow them, so *DO NOT* leave them around, *KEEP THEM IN A SAFE PLACE.* Cooper, being a puppy, might be tempted to eat one. This applies to everyone so I hope you are listening carefully!" he said, with a very serious tone in his voice!

Mum had been busy most of the morning preparing the Christmas dinner, and said to Dad, "Can you and the children tidy up and lay the dinner table please?"

“Yes Mum, we’d love to do that, come on kids let’s all work together as a team,” said Dad.
When they had finished Mum walked into the room and was pleasantly surprised. “Oh, WOW! the table looks very ‘Christmassy’ with the red tablecloth, serviettes and crackers. Thank you Dad and children, that’s a big help to me!!
Can you make sure that you put all the paper and packaging being thrown away, into the correct re-cycling bins, as we must all help to look after our planet? Did you see on the TV the ‘*billions of tons of plastic'* that ends up in the sea? The fish are eating it and the dolphins and whales are getting entangled in it! We have to take this massive problem seriously!” she said.

“Yes Mum, and did you see David Attenborough's Programme, Blue Planet Two?” asked Harry.
"It was AAAMMMAAAZZZIIINNNGGG!!! Anyone of us can get involved with conservation; if you go onto the TV website you can become an ‘OCEAN HERO’!!
“That sounds really interesting Harry, we will look into that for you,” said Dad.

Because I had been woken up so early I was feeling very tired, so I decided to curl up in my basket and I was just having a nice sleep, when, my nose picked up an amazing smell and my mouth began to drool.

I look up and the family are all sitting at the dinner table enjoying a delicious Christmas dinner. WOWEE! It looks very colourful with carrots, brussel sprouts, red cabbage, roast turkey, potatoes and lots of trimmings. My nose smelled every scent that came my way.

Where's mine? I think to myself.
Then Mum appears with a miniature Christmas dinner in my new stainless steel bowl with my name on it. There is just the right amount of food for my little body, and I hear Grandma say, "It's good to watch his portion size as we don't want him to get chubby, do we?"
I thought my tail was going to drop off! I couldn't stop wagging it at the sight and smell of my dinner. Dad asked if it was safe to give me some of their food as he had read that some human foods are poisonous to dogs! Grandma said, "Yes you do have to be careful, I have done my research and he can't have anything with onions in it, so you have to avoid gravy and stuffing,

and it's a definite 'NO' to Christmas pudding, mince pies, ice cream or chocolate."
I had a three-course dinner – melon, lots of turkey meat, a small amount of potato and vegetables and a slice of apple for my pudding. It was very tasty; I licked my bowl clean and drank my water.

Grandma said, "Good boy Cooper," and whispered in my ear, "You have had all of your 5-a-day in one meal, that's brilliant! You will be a healthy boy!"

After dinner, I noticed Harry and Kate were very thoughtful and helped the grownups to clear the table and tidy up. I thought, *that's good teamwork, I wonder if they always help?*

The family then spent time together looking at their presents. Kate had a joke book and everyone took it in turns to tell a joke. They were all helpless with laughter, especially when it was Harry's turn. "How come we laugh more at your jokes Harry?" asked Kate. "It's the way I tell 'em!" Said Harry.

Here are some of Kate's favourite jokes: -

Q. Where do fish keep their money?
A. In the riverbank!

Q. Who hides in the bakery during Christmas?
A. A mince spy!

Q. Why did the man run around his bed?
A. Because he was trying to catch up on his sleep!

Q. What runs, but never walks, often murmurs – never talks, has a bed but never sleeps, has a mouth but never eats? "I know this isn't a joke but I like it!" says Kate
A. A river!

Q. Why couldn't the pirates play cards?
A. Because the captain was standing on the deck!

6. Walkies in the Park

Later on Dad said, “Come on everyone we are taking Cooper for a walk in the park, we can all get some fresh air and exercise.”
“Cooper can’t go out until he has had his final vaccinations,” said Grandma.
“Oh, that’s OK, I will tuck him inside my jacket and carry him then,” said Dad.

I look rather smart wearing my silver and diamante collar, although I do feel that it is a bit ‘flashy’ for me. Grandma said I had to wear it because her friend Maggie had bought it especially for me for Christmas.

This is my first time out to socialise and we meet lots of people in the park, ‘walking off their Christmas

dinner'. Everyone is in a festive mood. I am still tucked inside Dad's jacket with my head poking out enjoying all the new sights and sounds. Families were stopping to stroke me with big smiles on their faces and they were asking if I was a Christmas present?
"He is so cute, will he always stay little like this?"
"No, he will treble in size!" said Dad.

The families were stroking and tickling me behind my ears. Harry and Kate loved showing me off and I loved all the attention.

There were children playing football and others riding their new bikes, and dogs racing around chasing each other. *One day soon I will be joining them,* I thought. *I can't wait! It looks like good fun!*

I notice that there are lots of bins in the park.
"Always put poo bags *IN THE BIN* and do not throw them anywhere on the floor," Dad said to Harry and Kate. "*THAT'S WHAT THE BINS ARE FOR!!!* But unfortunately there are thoughtless people who do throw the poo bags anywhere, they are in the minority, so just make sure you are not one of them," he said. Uugghh!! Stinky poo!!

"He's going to need puppy training lessons soon," said Dad. I thought, *that sounds good because I can meet lots of other puppies and you never know my brothers might be there! Oh, that would be nice wouldn't it?*

"How much will the lessons cost?" asks Mum.

Dad said quietly, "Cooper is an expensive Christmas present and everything could cost a lot of money."

I thought to myself, *I'm only little, how can I cost a lot of money?*

Dad said that in order to keep a dog clean, healthy and happy, you have to consider food, bedding, clothing, micro-chipping, pet insurance, flea and worming treatment, grooming, puppy training classes (if they

can afford them), making the garden secure so I don't escape, etc. etc.
Ooh La La – all of this makes you realise just how carefully you have to think, before you consider having a puppy like me. I thought.

Then Mum said, "I've got a good idea! I'll buy a piggy bank from the charity shop and we can put money in it every week to cover all of these expenses."
I thought to myself – *that* ***does*** *sound like a good idea, forward planning will give them a better chance of being able to afford me! What do you think?*

After all of the fresh air and excitement in the park I feel tired, but the children still want to play. I really need my sleep as I am still only a puppy and puppies do sleep a lot. As soon as we get back home, Grandma gently puts me in my basket.

"You have a nice snooze Cooper," she said. I fall fast asleep feeling very safe, warm and wanted.

7. Curtis the Cat

Suddenly I wake up to a strange hissing sound and see two huge green eyes glaring down at me from halfway up the stairs. It's a big ginger cat!

The cat slowly creeps down the stairs and watches me with every step it takes. My natural instinct wants to chase it. I can't really tell if the cat is scared of me, but it quickly runs into the kitchen and jumps on top of the cupboard where I think it feels safe.
The cat never takes its eyes off me!

Grandma picks me up and puts me on her knee and tells me quietly, ‘not to chase the cat’, whose name I learn is ‘Curtis’. But I can’t help it if my natural instinct tells me to chase cats, can I?

Grandma demonstrates to the family how to stroke me in one direction. She said, “You start at Cooper’s head and gently stroke down to his tail.”

Oh Grandma this gentle stroking is sooooooo relaxing I’m drifting into the land of nod!! I love it! I thought.

“Cooper will be a handful while he’s a puppy, but, with good training and socialising, he will become a good boy. It will be hard work for everyone but well worth it in the end.”

8. Oops who chewed Dad's Trainers?

I realise I need a wee so I get off Grandma's knee and wee on the carpet. I am immediately taken outside into the garden. I think this is part of my training. While I am thinking about this training, I have another wee in the garden and spy Dad's new Christmas trainers by the back door. *They look tasty.* I thought.

A little while later the children come to bring me inside and they are HORRIFIED to see that I have chewed one of the trainers…

"WHAT IS DAD GOING TO SAY? HE WILL GO BALLISTIC!!" Cry the children.

I don't understand why they are so worried; I wasn't hungry, but somehow, chewing the trainer did help ease the pain in my gums. I think I must be teething.

How am I to know that Dad's trainer is not the same as a toy? I have not been trained yet! Oh dear, I will learn in time the difference between right and wrong and what I can and cannot do… I promise!

Harry and Kate feel frightened thinking about how they are going to let Dad know about his chewed trainer?

Well, when Dad saw the state of his trainer he wasn't happy at all, and raised his voice, "WHAT'S GOING ON?" he shouted. "LOOK AT MY TRAINER!!"
This shouting really frightened me, I started trembling and my curly tail tucked itself tightly, in between my legs.

Mum said, “He is only a puppy and it’s the family’s job to train him as soon as possible. We are Cooper’s bosses and we have to be patient and persistent. We mustn’t shout at him when he does something wrong, but praise him when he does something right!!”
Yes, you are my bosses and if you train me, I will become a good boy. I thought.

Naturally, I wasn’t in Dad’s good books, and later on I had another accident in the kitchen but this time it was a runny poo, and guess what? Harry stepped in it, in his trainers, and walked into the lounge.

Uugghh! The stinky poo got stuck in the grooves on the soles of his trainers, which left an imprint pattern on the carpet. *How do you clean between the grooves?* I thought, *and how do you clean the carpet?*
I then hear Dad shout, "TAKE THE TRAINER OUTSIDE AND GET THE HOSEPIPE OUT..... QQUUIICCKK!"

Tempers started to flare. I was so frightened that I pooed again! All this shouting is making me shake all over and I am losing my confidence.

Then, I thought - *do you know that when poo is runny, it can get stuck to my curly coat, and you might have to wipe my bottom!! YIKES!! What do you think about that? Stinky poo!!*

I started thinking about my doggie family, where no one shouted when we had a wee or poo on the floor. I wondered *what are they doing now, are they missing me and when will I see them again?* Tears begin to roll down my face at the thought of them.

Maybe Grandma will take me to visit them one day, but for now I must try to enjoy my new home, garden and family, so I gently wipe my salty tears with my paw and join Harry and Kate who are watching television.

9. A dog is for Life not just for Christmas

All of a sudden something catches my eye on the television – a lot of sad looking puppies, crying with their tails tucked between their legs, flashes up on the TV screen. I am so exhausted from crying, that my eyes are closing, but I think to myself, *Cooper wake up, you had better watch this, as you never know, one of your brothers might be amongst them.*

They were being taken into a big building that said **RESCUE CENTRE.**

There were hundreds of them!! And I couldn't believe my eyes.

It was an advert showing puppies being taken to the Rescue Centre after Christmas last year. They looked traumatised and I felt soooooo sad for them.

RESCUE CENTRE

Apparently their new owners couldn't look after them properly. It was simply too much for them so they took them to the Rescue Centre.

- The wee, poo and sick
- Chewing everything
- Barking and whining
- Taking them for regular walks, especially on wet, muddy days
- Training classes (if you can afford them)
- Brushing them everyday
- Finding extra money to pay for everything
- Fitting it all in, around school and work

They had just thought of a cute, cuddly, playful puppy living with the family 'happily ever after'. But in real life there are always some problems that have to be worked out.

I look at the TV again and it now says: -

A DOG IS FOR LIFE NOT JUST FOR CHRISTMAS

The advert pointed out that nearly 4 puppies out of every 10 end up at the Rescue Centre to be re-homed!!

I thought, *oh dear, I hope that doesn't happen to me, I had better be on my best behaviour for Mum and Dad, but that's difficult when you are a puppy because they are your boss and if they don't train you, how can you learn?*

You simply don't stand a chance if your new owner doesn't train you, do you?

I've got to make them like me a lot so they never want to part with me. I promise I will listen and do everything they ask me.

Grandma joins us and I roll over onto my back for her to stroke and tickle me. When she stops, I prod her with my front paws and look into her eyes, pleading for more. She gets the message and carries on tickling me. Harry and Kate say, “Can we tickle him Grandma?”
“Yes, but be gentle, and one person at a time! Dogs don’t like more than one person fussing over them. They can become nervous, and because they can’t talk, they may even snap at you; if they do snap or nip you, this can be their way of telling you to ‘*leave them alone’* as it’s too much for them. Most dogs like being tickled and cuddled, but remember - only by one person at a time!” she said.

10. The Football Match

Once everything was cleaned up and back to normal the family sat down to enjoy the evening. The conversation was mainly about football, which put Dad in a good mood, 'thank goodness'.
"I've got a nice surprise for you kids for tomorrow."
"Oh, what's that Dad?"
"Well, it's tradition to support your local football team on Boxing Day, so I am treating all of us to go to the big match."
"Who are we going to see?"
"My favourite team, Bradley Rovers."
"Wow! Thanks Dad, what a great surprise! We will really look forward to that!"

Everyone was feeling tired after all of the excitement of Christmas day, especially Cooper!
"Let's have an early night so we will have plenty of energy to walk to the match tomorrow. Come on kids, *up the apple and pears (stairs),*" said Dad.
Everyone kissed and cuddled me and said, "Goodnight puppy Cooper, sleep tight."
This made me feel soooooooooooo good!!

Before Mum went to bed, she put extra paper on the floor in case I went to the toilet in the night. She wagged her finger at me and said, “If you have a wee or a poo Cooper, please try and go on the paper.” Then she blew me a kiss.

I get the feeling that she understands that it will take time for me to learn all of these good habits.

I cried myself to sleep again! *I wonder - when am I going to stop crying? I heard Mum say ‘it could take at least a week for me to settle in!’*

MATCH DAY

Next day Grandma and I waved the family goodbye as they went off to the match. Harry and Kate were very excited!

They were all dressed in warm clothing as ‘Jack Frost’ had been out in the night, and it was a bit chilly. They had their Bradley Rover’s black and white striped scarves around their necks to keep them snug.

I wished I was going with them. I thought.

Let's hope they win!
Up the Rovers... Up the Rovers!

When I was in the kitchen this morning, just before they left, I was being a bit nosey, and I heard it mentioned that Grandma was going home in two days time, as she was only staying here for Christmas.
I am going to really miss her! I thought.

Now I was alone with Grandma, I sat and looked into her eyes with a worried expression; She must have known what I was thinking because she said, "Don't worry Cooper, you will be seeing a lot of me when I 'puppy sit'. You will be coming to stay with me at my house every Tuesday whilst your Mum and Dad go to work and the children are at school.
I don't live far away and there is a big park and river where I will be taking you to explore. There are all kinds of dogs there for you to tease and run around with… and squirrels too!"
That sounds good, as I love having fun. I thought.
"We can call at the café for a sandwich and a drink, and if the weather is ok we can sit outside, get some fresh air, and share a bit of gossip with the other owners and their dogs."

Ooh, I like the sound of all that! I thought.

After the match the family arrived home with rosy cheeks and looking sooooooo happy!
Harry and Kate burst through the door shouting, "THEY WON!! THEY WON!! And they scored a penalty! We've had an amazing time Grandma. Dad's team were ace and there were lots of goals, lots of people, and we had lots of fun!"
"What was the score, then?" asked Grandma.
"It was 3:2 Grandma."
"WOW!! That sounds like a thrilling match Dad took you to see," she replied.

Kate and Harry said, "We want to thank you Dad for treating us, and, we have a big question to ask you, WHEN CAN WE GO AGAIN?"
"We'll have to think about that kids, as we need to save some pennies first."
"OK Dad, what about if we do some jobs to earn some pocket money?" They eagerly ask.
"Yes, that's a good idea kids. I've got lots of jobs you can help me and Mum with, you can make a New Years resolution and start on the 1st of January."

"YYYYEEEESSSS!!!!!!!!! The sooner the better so we can go to watch Bradley Rovers again!!"

The whole family gave a 'high-five'.
They were soooooooooo Happy!!!

*****